Thunder Over The Door

Of Boats and Bays and Fir-Clad Bluffs

Robert Dickson Murray

Wm Caxton Ltd
Ellison Bay, Wisconsin

Published by

Wm Caxton Ltd
12037 Highway 42
Ellison Bay, WI 54210

(414) 854-2955

Printed in the United States of America.

10 9 8 7 6 5 4 3 2 1

Library of Congress Cataloging-in-Publication Data

Murray, Robert Dickson, 1906-1991.
    Thunder over the Door : of boats and bays and fir-clad bluffs / Robert Dickson
Murray.
      p. cm.
    Includes index.
    ISBN 0-940473-22-4 (alk. paper) : $19.95
    1. Ellison Bay (Wis.)--Description. 2. Murray, Robert Dickson, 1906-1991. 3. Door
County (Wis)--Discription and travel.
    I. Title.
F589.E45M87 1991
917.75'63--dc20   91-16418
                                                               CIP

ISBN# 0-940473-22-4

This book is set in a version of Palatino type chosen for its readability and attractiveness; it is printed on acid-neutral paper bound in sewn signatures and is intended to provide a very long useful life.

Table of Contents

To

Bettina Woolverton Murray

my greatest love
and constant inspiration.

Foreword

In the late 1800s, the beautiful body of water known as Green Bay was remote, isolated, and hard to get to. French explorers had given the name *Porte des Morts* ("door of the dead") to the stretch of water between the north end of the Door County peninsula and Washington Island, and the numerous remains of ships that litter the beaches and bottom of the passage bear witness to the accuracy of its title. The name was anglicized to "Death's Door" or simply "the Door," and Door County is named for it.

Porte des Morts remains a treacherous and dangerous passage. The violence and beauty of the thunderstorms that sometimes sweep through the Door are amazing and unforgettable, and they can send an unwary captain onto the rocks before he realizes he is in danger. When thunderheads form over the Door, small craft head for shelter. Even large ships sometimes seek shelter in the lee of the peninsula rather than brave the Door in a storm.

By the turn of the century, the Chicago and Northwestern Railroad was a pretty classy way to travel to the city of Green Bay from Chicago or Milwaukee, but from there on, transport up the Door County peninsula was primitive at best. The Green Bay and Western Railroad went as far as Sturgeon Bay carrying mainly freight — bulk, package, and some cattle, but cow by cow, not herd by herd — and only a few passengers. North of Sturgeon Bay, the rural mail truck was the only alternative to horse and wagon, if traveling by land. Small steamers plied the waters of Green Bay, but they offered rather spartan accommodations and few, if any, schedules.

Then, in 1906, the Goodrich Company in Chicago sent their newly acquired, newly rebuilt steamship *Carolina* up to the turquoise waters of Green Bay via the Sturgeon Bay ship canal and on to Mackinac Island, through the Door. Returning via the same route gave her a round trip each week from late June until early September, and it gave Door County a luxury way to go.

For nearly thirty years the *Carolina* kept this schedule every week, every summer. Then in 1935 she was sold! In 1950 the last of her sleek, black hull was cut up for scrap metal. But the *Carolina* still lives in pictures, in the written word, and in the memories of the elderly, for she was an integral part of Door County's growing up.

Carolina also left her voice — a soft alto chord, low pitched and mellifluent. You used to be able to hear it across the bluffs before she came into view, and again a little later when she saluted the dock. On a summer's evening, if you go down to where Roeser's dock was, you might be able to hear its haunting echo even now.

The transcendent voices of northeastern Wisconsin? A long-gone steamship's whistle . . . and Thunder Over the Door.

Chapter 1
Tenero

Beautiful, remote, naive. Limestone bluffs jut skyward on one side; silken sand beaches on the other. Sentinel firs stand at attention, while white birches, oaks, and maples blend their feathery grace into a natural elegance. Where there are open fields, stones are the predominant crop, shining white in the high sun. The surrounding waters are Mediterranean blue, clear, clean, and fresh. To the east, Lake Michigan hems the shore in lacy white; on the west, the blue-green deeps of Green Bay edge right up to the shore. This is the Door County Peninsula, thumb of Wisconsin's hand stretched out in welcome to the world.

A likely lass she is, sweet, innocent, and lovely. But, back when the twentieth century began, she recognized her own beauty only in the number of logs moved out and the number of fish brought in. That, was early, when she was very young, when split logs cooked and heated, when dinner was always at noon, when country stores dealt in basics.

Then great orchards of sour, red cherries began to spring up and burgeon. They replaced lumbering, so long preeminent, even as the clear, clean waters gradually were stripped of their trout and as whitefish fell prey to voracious lamprey eels swimming upstream from salt water. The red cherries flourished, rivaling the production of Michigan's orchards, and you could buy canned cherries from Door County almost anywhere.

But, alas, people crowded out some of the red-cherry orchards, replacing them with real-estate developments. Motels and cottages for rent sprang up; water-front property became valuable, and there was none to buy. Where dinner used to be at noon, now supper clubs offered gourmet dining well into the night, and sophisticated lounges with exotic and tempting drinks relegated nineteenth-century saloons and beer parlors to an almost forgotten past. The tranquility of each curving bay, once echoing only to the chug of a fishing boat, a steamer's whistle, or the chuckle of waves, now reverberates to the staccato outboard, to the crisp curling slap from the curling wake of water skiers, and to the silence left behind by wind surfers.

The privy has been replaced by the flush john.

Is this bad? Of course not. What once was enjoyed by a few under spartan conditions is now a playground for many. The rest is the same — clear blue water, sentinel pines, and exquisite scenery. Door County, now a mature beauty, has emerged from her early naivete into a world of greater sophistication. She prospers as never before, and she does so serenely and with immanent grace.

Back around 1911, when the lumber industry in Door County was on the wane and commercial fishing was reaching its zenith, vacationers were an oddity in the northern part of the peninsula. Fish Creek and Ephraim catered to a few, but, in the main, visitors were traveling salesmen. They usually braved the rigors of the area twice a year — in spring after the snow was gone and the water was clear of ice, and in autumn before the ermine mantle of winter covered the greenery and clogged such roads as there were.

On his return to Chicago from such a trip in the fall of 1911, a traveling salesman representing Hibbard, Spencer, Bartlett & Company, wholesale hardware merchants in Chicago, extolled the beauties of Door County to a friend. The virtues of Chicago in the summer were practically nil and those of southern Michigan very little better, and so his stories of crisp cool nights, hot dry days, and succulent salmon trout appealed. He explained to his friend that getting to Door County was not what he would call easy. He rode the Chicago and Northwestern Railway to the city of Green Bay, where he boarded one of the small steamers sailing north up Green Bay to wherever freight was waiting to be moved. Quarters on the

Bon Ami, the *Sailor Boy*, and the *Thistle* were not luxurious — even mere comfort was an iffy proposition — but they were solid little ships, and they always got where they were going. That is, two of them did. *Thistle* was much older and less robust than the others, and she had a tendency to snuggle down on the bottom if she was left unattended at her dock too long.

S.S. Bon Ami approaching Ephraim dock 1913

On the other hand, the salesman recommended the Goodrich Transit Company steamer which sailed directly from Chicago to the peninsula. It usually took a little longer to get there, but it was well worth it.

Thus, in the early summer of 1912, a love story began between a six-year-old boy and the *Carolina*, a ship, a boat, a steamer. The *Carolina* was female (as all ships are), beautiful, poised, and a little arrogant (as many ladies appear to be). At first, the boy was shy and worshipped this new love with his eyes alone. But later, he could admit his love even to himself, for he found that she returned his affection in full. Like so many other things about the *Carolina*, the boy found this new emotion strange and wonderful, and it remained wonderful, though no longer strange, as he kept it inside of him, all to himself.

The *Sailor Boy*

Many people were fond of the *Carolina*, and some may even have been as fond of her as was the six-year-old boy. But that's doubtful, for the love he had for her remains as real today as it was then, though over seventy years have passed and she, the *Carolina*, was cut up for scrap metal more than half a century ago.

The *Carolina* was a sleek 223 feet long, with a crisply black hull and sparkling white superstructure. Amidships, her bright red funnel was topped with a wide band of black, and her gaff-topped masts were canted aft just enough to suggest a touch of vanity. She tossed black smoke from her funnel as a young girl might flaunt her curls.

Thistle

Historically, steamship whistles were a deep, authoritative bass. But, back at the turn of the century, someone with both imagination and the soul of a poet (or perhaps, a musician) chose to create a melodious sound, a contralto chord, perfect in pitch and hauntingly feminine, for *Carolina's* whistle. To those on deck below, her whistle was indeed fortissimo, but beautifully so. From a distance, near or far, it was enchanting, for it held within its tone a promise of faraway places, of romance, and of urgency. It was always perfect — no blowing off of excess steam before the true tone emerged — and, from its opening note, it tempted its listeners much as Lorelei did, but with a promise of delight rather than of destruction.

It is strange to look back on that day-and-a-half adventure cruise aboard the *Carolina* and to realize that the same distance to the same place now can be covered by automobile in a half day. From big city to deep woods, with a stop at Smith's in Port Washington for lunch, and you're there. It is sad that there now is no choice; the *Carolina* and the other ships like her are only memories that can be revived now and then by old photographs or paintings. But perhaps the metal from the *Carolina* is included in the frame of the soaring building where your office is, or in the body of your automobile. Let's hope the latter, for hers was a moving life.

There was nothing like the fresh lake air, the gentle motion, and the sense of having nothing whatsoever to do while on board. And there was the excitement of each port of call, each fending breakwater, each harbor light, the melody of her whistle sending chills up and down your imagination, the anticipation of being served in the elegant dining salon and then — the final delight — falling asleep before you knew it to the whisper of the lake wind and the hiss of her wake cascading out and away. The breeze from shore brought the scent of pine and cedar as the turbid smell of hot city streets faded in memory. And there was time — time to take it all in, to take it all in and to savor it — to realize that it was happening to you right now.

The *Carolina* sailed from the foot of Rush Street in Chicago, just beyond the bridge at one o'clock on a day early in July of 1912, or 1913, or 1914 . . . or whenever. The odor of roasting coffee combined with the fumes off the Chicago River, but both were dissipated by a friendly lake breeze before they became objectionable.

Above, on the starboard bridge jutting out from the pilot house, a man appeared. He was short and plump, and he wore an elfin smile as well as a captain's uniform. This was Daniel J. McGarity, master of the steamship *Carolina* as well as all he surveyed. He sent his orders to the engine room below by virtue of shrieks from two whistles attached to the bridge, one at either hand. The higher shriek asked for slow ahead on the starboard screw. A slight quiver along her entire length was evidence that this command was being carried out, and the gap between the *Carolina*'s black hull and the creaking wharf widened. Another shriek, this one in a lower tone, brought an additional quiver, and the wharf began slipping astern, for now the port screw had added its slow-ahead thrust, and our forward motion was established. From his post on the bridge, Captain McGarity looked fore and aft, and, satisfied that all was in order, he gave one last glance astern before repairing to his place on the part of the bridge just in front of the pilot house. The shriek whistles at the ends of the wings of the bridge were now abandoned, and Captain McGarity placed himself between two consoles — one for each engine — and used them to signal his orders below. Unlike the startling whistles, the consoles sent orders with a quiet "dr-r-ring" and received replies in the same subtle tone. Both engines were now proceeding at "half ahead."

On the left, to port, the then-new Municipal Pier of Chicago slipped by. To starboard, low sheds and small buildings edged the river and the lakefront swept away to the south. The sky was crisp blue, the clouds billowing cumulus.

Once clear of Chicago's breakwater, the "dr-r-ring" sounded again, and both engines began to throb at full ahead. The bow wave became more interesting, tossing ever higher cascades of turquoise water into splashing white foam as the *Carolina*'s forward thrust increased. At last, Captain McGarity swung his ship in a long arc to port, up-lake, and set his course for Milwaukee, ninety miles away. The departure was a jumble of impressions. Only afterwards did things began to sort themselves out — things like a ship, which is inanimate but nevertheless seems to have a soul of its own.

As the ship sailed north toward Milwaukee along the Illinois-Wisconsin shore, she edged farther and farther out into the lake until land became simply a hazy line along the horizon. Deck chairs had been found and claimed, some pulled out toward the rail, others left in the shade of the deck above. Adults found the rigors of business being diluted by the steady, cool breeze and the wash of water cascading astern. Some contributed to the low hum of conversation; others were lulled by it. But there was also the scamper of feet along the decks to add a little percussion to the music of wind and waves and talk.

The sun, which had been overhead at departure, now bathed the port deck in its glare; the other side was in shadow and distinctly cooler. Standing in the glare, you found the *Carolina* much closer in to shore, and you might even pick out the chimneys of Racine, back a little, punctuating its lines of buildings.

But hold on here! A gong was sounding. A man in a white jacket was playing his chimes as he walked about the deck.

Dinner in fifteen minutes!

There was a rush for the cabins to be first at the wash stand and mirror.

Dinner in the dining salon! An event! And it was elegant. the Maitre d' was a huge man with a professional smile and a ring with a diamond as big as a small boy's imagination. He seated everyone and hovered about, making sure that every diner enjoyed the menu as well as the view through the many windows. Lake Michigan furnished the whitefish and trout, Wisconsin provided the chicken, and Chicago contributed steaks and roast beef. In that day and time the fish were fresh, the chickens plump, and the beef had been allowed to hang for the right amount of time at the right temperature to achieve the ultimate in flavor.

Gorged and sated, or at least satisfied, the passengers once again crowded onto the decks, for the *Carolina* was about to pass the gap in the breakwater and enter Milwaukee's harbor. At reduced speed, Captain McGarity guided his charge into the Milwaukee River. Bridges lifted their arms to heaven at the behest of *Carolina*'s melodious whistle, while he slipped her through the narrow spaces. Where the river forked, the Captain spun his ship slowly around, one propeller driving forward, the other pulling aft, and guided her to her mooring at the foot of Michigan Street.

It was deep night now. Much freight had been unloaded, and other freight had replaced it in the hold. Some passengers had disembarked, others had come aboard. Finally, activity began in the pilot house which brought immediate responses in the engine room, at the gangways, and at the mooring ropes which held the ship to the dock.

The forward gangplank was pulled aboard and the hatch closed. A dr-r-r-ing from overhead preceded a shiver along the *Carolina*'s length, and the passenger gangway was pulled aboard. Captain McGarity took the starboard bridge, and the whistle shrieked two orders to the engine room. It was eleven at night, but the whistles and shouting and motion wakened no one, for no one had gone to bed. Not on this night. Young and old lined the decks, watching as black water separated the *Carolina* from her berth. Her resonant whistle called with all the harmonious beauty of a symphony for the first bridge to open, and then to another, and another. No more shrieks issued from the wing bridges, for Captain McGarity had taken his stand between the consoles forward of the pilot house, but there were numerous dr-r-r-ings, as he signaled the engine room.

The Milwaukee River was lined with lights on warehouses, streets, and bridges, but at last the final bridge raised its arms and released the outbound *Carolina* to her rightful milieu, the open lake. It was like going into the unknown. Lights showed only here and there along the breakwater to either side and in a small cluster at the harbor entrance. Beyond that was only black night, black water, and stars. Then, as a final dr-r-r-ing sent the

Carolina to full ahead, her white wake began to spread out on either side, looking for all the world like agitated ghosts dematerializing as they fell away astern.

The wind freshened just before midnight. Could it be a precursor of rough seas ahead? But it stayed fresh, and our apprehension abated. The ghostly wake danced as before, and yawns began to mark the end of a very full day for everyone.

As Captain McGarity turned the *Carolina* north into the night, we sought our cabins. Ours was on the forward hurricane deck, just aft of Captain McGarity's domain, just forward of the green starboard light, and we imagined we could hear the captain moving about next door. We could see a touch of green from the light reflected on the jamb of our window, which was open to the freshening breeze.

To sleep on a moving ship; to savor the cool, crisp lake air; to feel the breeze washing the cabin; to hear the muted sound of the wake tumbling below; to know utter childlike confidence in the ship itself and in Captain McGarity — that was indeed to dream.

✠ ✠ ✠

The *Carolina* was on the Green Bay/Mackinaw run from 1906 until about 1931, but it was the thirteen years between 1914 and 1927 in which she was supreme. Those were the years when her master was Daniel McGarity, and, during each of those summers, the *Carolina* seemed delighted to be under his guidance.

Each year, the *Carolina* was taken out of service during the winter months, and during that time Captain McGarity mastered the ice-breaking *SS Alabama*. Usually, it was in mid-June each year that you first could see the *Carolina* clearing the Sturgeon Bay canal with a cargo of passengers and freight for Door County. Through the canal she sailed, and north up Green

Bay. The *Carolina* was Captain McGarity's first love, and their reunion each spring, each year for fourteen springs, was always something more than routine.

McGarity was part and parcel of the *Carolina*. His Irish smile seemed as much a part of the ship as her funnels. His private deck extended forward of the pilot house and ended in two wing bridges, one to port and one to starboard. From there he reigned over his domain, handling the two engines belowdecks with the gentle persuasiveness of a lover, keeping watch on changing weather with respect and anticipation. He demanded and got the full allegiance of his crew. He was the soul and master of the *Carolina*, as well as her eyes and ears.

Daniel J. McGarity
Captain
S.S. Carolina 1914-1927

McGarity wore his Captain's cap jauntily on one side, and he strutted the bridge of his command with absolute confidence and supreme pride. The ship responded in kind. Their rapport was such that Captain McGarity once took her up the tortuous Milwaukee River, through numerous bridges raised at the behest of her beautifully chimed whistle, turned her about in the basin and docked her — all without benefit of her rudder, which had become locked in a dead astern position. Now *that* was handling 220 feet of dead tonnage with finesse!

If Daniel McGarity was the soul and master of his beloved *Carolina*, she was his mistress.

Chapter 2
Allegro

The cacophony of making port in Manitowoc failed to waken most of the passengers. They had retired late the night before, their lungs full of lake-washed air, and the abundant oxygen had had its narcotic effect. It was now early in the morning, around six. But, once the motion of the ship ceased — like that — it was as if an alarm clock had gone off.

The tempo of the new day was more excited than before. Yesterday had been languid, at peace with the world; falling into a cool, clean berth had been a fitting finale, and tomorrow had seemed an infinity away. But tomorrow was here, crisp and clear. The decks of the *Carolina* had been washed down overnight, and the ship sparkled in the morning sun.

There was much to do. Breakfast was a feast, from prosaic oatmeal and prunes, to smokey bacon and golden cornmeal pancakes. Sea-air appetites made even the prunes sweeter. At that time, prunes were the breakfast fruit; frozen sun-golden orange juice was not yet available, and grapefruit was out of season for the summer. But, even before breakfast, there was the fascinating business of getting the *Carolina* out into the lake and turning her north once more.

The next port-of-call would be Kewaunee, a short stop. There, the main road swept up the hill to the right, the town lay straight ahead to the left, and two car ferries made ready to sail — one to Frankfort, the other to Ludington, both in Michigan across the way.

Once beyond Kewaunee, the *Carolina* buffeted its way up the lake toward Algoma, where a red lighthouse marked the entrance to a harbor that narrowed and became the Ahnapee River. The Ahnapee is short, but it abounded in bulrushes where bass lay in wait, and there was once a railroad named after it, the Ahnapee and Western. The river terminates fifteen miles upstream, and the railroad extended only twenty-odd miles to

Sturgeon Bay. But, anyone who has fished the Ahnapee and ridden the railroad knows that they were an integral part of Door County.

Algoma itself was and is a lovely little town. On one side, a red church spire marked the piety of the townsfolk, while the woodworking plant along the north bank of the Ahnapee, just over the bridge from the center of town, was mute evidence of its industrious ways. If memory serves, the plant was owned by the Church Company, and it claimed to manufacture the "Most Important Seat In The House." South of the river, tree-shaded streets beckoned, for the heat of midday was almost at hand.

Once clear of the red lighthouse at the harbor entrance, a waiter strolling with the gong advised passengers that lunch was being served in the dining salon. This would be the last meal aboard for those disembarking at Door County ports.

It seemed to one and all that the morning had simply raced by. For some, a sort of panic set in; the cruise was too rapidly nearing its end. Many hurried their last luncheon in order not to miss the scenery, the strange and delightful smells, or the excitement on deck — like when Captain McGarity reduced speed to "slow ahead" as he approached the entrance to the Sturgeon Bay ship canal; like watching the bow sweep its dancing wake against the canal pilings in diminishing scallops; like watching the canal grow wider as we approached it from the lake; like waving to fishermen along the canal who seemed undecided whether to resent the disruption or to thrill to her progress through the canal, long, sleek, and arrogant.

Sturgeon Bay itself opened up before us. On the left, the town of Sawyer, on the right, the city of Sturgeon Bay, county seat of Door County with its shipyards on beyond. Between Sturgeon Bay and Sawyer there was a swing bridge, but the *Carolina* pulled in at the wharf along the shore before reaching it.

S.S. Carolina northbound out of Sturgeon Bay 1915

While we were still tied up at the wharf, Captain McGarity called upon the bridge to swing upon its pivot and let the *Carolina* through. Three long melodious chords from the ship's whistle were the signal, and they were so enchanting that folks along the shore and in the two towns hesitated for just a moment to relish its challenge to go . . . off to seek adventure. The bridge responded by beginning its slow swing, and the *Carolina* cast off the fetters holding her wharfside and headed down the bay, slipping gracefully through the limited space granted here before passing to the wider reaches of the long bay.

S.S. Carolina Algoma 1919

Almost at once there was a change. The bay seemed greener and deeper in color than the lake had. Small whitecaps came charging menacingly down at us. Wind clouds gathered and encouraged the whitecaps to grow. The fragrance of cedar wafted over us, and rocks jutted along the shore where there had been sand on the lake side. But the *Carolina*, now at full speed ahead, cast the small whitecaps to either side, as her captain began the long swing to the north, out into the choppy water of Green Bay. The Green Bay side of Door County now lay ahead off our starboard bow. Limestone bluffs laden with cedar, pine, balsam, and spruce

S.S. Carolina Sister Bay 1926

rose out of stone beaches jutting out from the shore. Around each bluff, was a more sheltered bay, usually with a village nestled at its head, complete with white church steeple piercing the green background and a dock with a red building aboard down front along the water.

The first village, Egg Harbor, was a ways up-bay, but we didn't stop. The *Carolina* just sailed on by until she rounded a low bluff and we found ourselves approaching Fish Creek. There was more *Carolina* than there was dock in Fish Creek, but Captain McGarity brought her up smartly, shrieked the engines to "full astern" and came to a stop at just the right place. The dock was crowded, for, just after rounding the point, the captain had called three times with his chimed whistle, and everything in town had stopped as everyone came down to see the Goodrich boat come in.

Some freight came off and several passengers disembarked before we were on our way again. We passed another stretch of rocky shore, this time culminating in a much higher bluff that we could look up to as we rounded it. Then, away down at the foot of this long bay lay the red Anderson Dock of Ephraim, flanked by white buildings and with that same deep background stretching away and beyond in both directions. *Carolina*'s whistle reverberated from high-rising Eagle bluff and danced its way to the other shore and back. The call went out in three alto chords, and the tocsin had been sounded. The boat from Chicago was in range, bearing the freight and friends and fantasies that she always brought.

It was the latter part of the afternoon now. Colors were intense. The stony shore sloped away to the north, and here and there a dock jutted out, some with fish boats moored to them, the type of boats that used to catch trout and whitefish commercially.

Farther north — much farther — a long line of shore rose gradually until it abruptly terminated in a most impressive cliff, but Sister Bay came first. We rounded another bluff behind which was tucked a lumber mill just beyond, and along to the left was the town itself. Not a big town, but it

S.S. Carolina leaving Sister Bay, 1922

seemed to spread out before becoming lost in the green of the firs growing so abundantly.

Again there was much scurrying around on the dock, for more people had reached their journey's end, and baggage had to be packed and sent down the gangway, ours among the rest.

Daniel J. McGarity could show off a bit here in Sister Bay, for the water became very deep very quickly, and the *Carolina's* twin screws bit into the dark green depths with authority as she came to a halt and was moored by her great ropes to the dock.

We were gathered below at the head of the forward gangway, since the *Carolina* was too long to get her passenger exit up to the small dock, and a feeling of utter and complete loss had begun to mount. Once on shore, we looked aloft and were saluted by Captain McGarity just before his signals shrieked their command to the engine room — "slow astern." Slowly, the *Carolina* began to back out. What tragedy! What devastation! At least so it seemed to one small boy who stood, slightly pigeon-toed, with his cap secured to his jacket by a black cord, as he watched his first love leave him, beautiful and arrogant, and growing smaller by the minute. He gave a small gesture of farewell, but she simply flaunted her white wake, tossed the black curls of her smoke, and went on her way.

Captain McGarity had left the wing bridge, and the *Carolina* was outbound for Washington Island and beyond.

Chapter 3
Transposition

With a growl and a snort our coach came to life; it was one of two motor-driven vehicles north of Sturgeon Bay in 1912, and it carried mail, passengers, and a little freight from Ellison Bay to Sturgeon Bay and back, every day except Sunday.

Walter C. Olson was to the motor-coach part of the transportation scene what Daniel J. McGarity was to his; he had come to the Goodrich dock to pick up a family of fugitives from the Chicago summer who, it had been rumored, would be aboard the boat. When he greeted us, his smile was big, his grip was firm, and therewith began a friendship that lasted as long as he lived. With a wave toward the north he told us, "Ellison Bay is just up yonder. Mrs. Anderson is expecting you at the Hillside Hotel. Now we'll load your trunks."

Did he say trunks? In that day and time, one did not pack a sleek suitcase and take along a dress or suit bag. One packed a trunk or two with everything from clothes to toilet paper, toothpaste, and crackers. Our trunks had been shipped out on the preceding trip of the Goodrich boat and awaited us near the door of the Sister Bay warehouse. It took almost all the space in Walter Olson's bus to transport our trunks, our grips, and us the five miles to Ellison Bay.

The air in this northern outpost was strange to us, strange and pleasant. The sawmill on the other end of the Sister Bay dock was working, and, as planks came off the line, they were loaded onto low-lying sailing vessels moored with masts sticking high and sails furled. The fragrance of the fresh-sawed pine was a feast of spicy pleasure accented by the odor of cedar trees on the bluff above.

As we set out for Ellison Bay, our final destination, even our brief contact with Sister Bay was temporarily lost. Mr. Olson's sturdy bus lumbered up the hill from the dock and sawmill to the main road and turned left toward the north once more. Then, suddenly, we found ourselves in the center of town. The General Store even then was Bunda's, and there was a meat market, a post office, and a saloon. Further up the road was a white hotel with a peaked roof and a sign that said "Liberty Grove Hotel." Then we laboriously climbed another hill, rounded a slight bend, and, at a dusty fifteen miles an hour, we were on our way.

We passed through a pastoral scene with groves of trees, fields, and white stone fences. Here and there a cow took advantage of the grass or the shade, while back among the trees a house and a barn and sheds could occasionally be made out. Once we saw a farmer plowing a field with his team, and further on, a flat grey wagon on which a few bags were piled stood idly by. A long way ahead, a strip of green — an island — lay across the horizon like a great crocodile asleep in the water.

But, where was Ellison Bay?

And then we found it! Walter Olson stopped his bus on the brink of a long hill. A blue-water bay curved below and beyond, the deep blue coming nearly to the shore before becoming the light green of shallows. A big, sturdy dock supporting two red buildings reached out into the blue water from the foot of the bay, and a long sweep of shore stretched away to the north until it became a point with a low bluff. The green foliage came down almost to the water but was separated from it by a stone beach. The beach glistened white in the afternoon sun, wide around the foot of the bay near the big dock, but narrowing as it swept out toward the north. In some spots, limestone rock pushed its way through the greenery into the open. Over the point, but before the sleeping crocodile, a larger bluff loomed in the middle distance.

A road led inland from the big dock to a group of buildings; that was the town. The road we were on curved to the right below us before correcting its course with a slight bend to the left. It led into town, but trees

Walter C. Olson's Stage Coach
Baileys Harbor 1913

and bushes obscured the buildings from where we stood. However, halfway down the hill was a building we could see clearly. Mr. Olson pointed it out as Mike Anderson's Hillside Hotel, where we were going to stay.

Below us and to the left was a grassy field with a number of cows edging their way toward a gate in anticipation of being herded home for evening milking. Further to the left beyond the field rose a bluff. A big bluff, a prominence, covered with the deep green of closely bunched trees. In truth, we stood on that bluff, while the pasture sloped down for a half-mile or so to the tree-lined shore like a natural stadium, with the field as the sweep of the stands and the jutting bluff the great buttress at the end.

And there, way, way out on Green Bay, was the *Carolina,* continuing on her way to enchantment, a wisp of black smoke staining the sky astern, white wake streaming along her black side, and sparkling superstructure glistening in the setting sun.

The boy, who had fallen in love with her and been saddened that she had not waved farewell to him, smiled. Surely that wisp of smoke gestured to him, barely apparent but enough to make him smile. And then he turned his attention to the sight below, where another love brazenly beckoned.

✣ ✣ ✣

In 1912, many of the fish houses were as weathered and gray as they are now, mute evidence of having been built in the last century. The breakwaters have protected them through many a winter and have fended off the spring ice floes bent on moving everything in their path out to Death's Door for demolition.

Originally, lighting for these shacks came exclusively from kerosene lamps, for much work was done at night. The boats brought in large catches of fish, and darkness was upon them when they came in. Later on, electric wires could be seen stretching inland, and flashlights replaced oil lanterns.

Ellison Bay Bluff 1912

As the fishing boats became larger and more efficient, these picturesque buildings became too small. Others were built in their stead — many with shingled siding and shingled roofs — and they were placed on larger cribs, instead of pilings, that were topped with concrete for easier walking. The older, more colorful buildings were retired to complete their lives as places of storage, sometimes to be pictured on postcards for the folks back home.

And then there were the icehouses, with the same weathered pine-wood sides, but open to the sky on top. Usually tucked into the trees on the perimeters of the fish-house clearings in order to avoid the direct rays of the sun, they were filled with sawdust and large chunks of ice cut from the adjacent bay in winter when the ice was thickest. In their secluded surroundings, with the ice deep in insulating sawdust, these icehouses kept the ice intact all summer.

✛ ✛ ✛

Johan Brendt Eliason settled at what is now Ellison Bay in about 1858. In 1873, he applied to establish a post office there, but the Postal Department had a rule that a post office could not be named after its postmaster. Thus, when the application was approved, some unknown hand in Washington D.C. dubbed it "Ellison" Bay to conform with the rule, and thus gave the settlement its name.

Between 1912 and 1928, Ellison Bay attracted quite a number of outlanders who bought properties, built on them, and returned to them every summer to settle their nerves, recharge their batteries, and generally prepare for the winter to come. They all paid taxes, some supported the church, and all patronized the local stores and other businesses. During July and August they became an integral part of the community.

Although there were some changes, like Helmer Bergman's garage and the Disgarden Hotel's new wing, Ellison Bay remained much the same

Eagle, Leo, G.H. Clayton, and *Ruby* tied up during a storm   1915

during that period. A few cottages were built back in the woods along the Little Bluff, and Charley Anderson's five-room house was converted into the sixteen-bedroom Ellison Bay Lodge by the Wickmans, Gilbert and Olga, but none of these altered the essence of the community.

Charles Ruckert's store was the center of town, and the building looks now almost exactly as it did in 1919. Fred Riding's blacksmith shop was across the intersection, catty corner from Ruckert's. A little further up the Rowleys Bay road was the church. The blacksmith shop and the old church are gone. This was before the time of the Viking Grill and its fish boils.

The handsome log house pictured on page 29 was built by Jens Jensen just north of Ellison Bay, before you get to Death's Door Bluff. Jensen was Consultant Landscape Architect for the Chicago park system, and he had found a little of his native Denmark in the rugged bluffs on the Green Bay side of Door County. In 1920, this "cottage" still stood, but it was destroyed by fire a few years later.

Jensen was finally able to rebuild it, and from then on his dream of a place where serious people could come and pursue studies of nature and the arts grew to fruition. He is gone now, but what he planned for the bluff overlooking Green Bay has become what he wanted it to be.

Jensen's home is just the sort of building that the early "outlanders" had or wanted. It was a showplace, and the Clearing introduced city conveniences where they had been thought unnecessary before. In fact, many of the outlanders preferred to struggle with Aladdin Filament lamps, to pump their water, and to bathe in the bay or lake. The sound at night of little waves on the stones was more welcome than the throb of a refrigerator, and the beat of rain on the roof was more soothing than no sound of rain at all. How better to appreciate the city than not to have it!

Jens Jensen's home "The Clearing" as it appeared in the early 1920s.

✛ ✛ ✛

One of the delights of the peninsula is the sight of the Lutheran Church as you approach Sister Bay from the north. The picture on page 31 was copied from a snapshot taken in 1919.

The photo shows a beautiful sight that can still be seen, but it also displays a road marker for Route 17. When Wisconsin first began to mark its roads, around 1915 or 1916, Route 17 started at the Illinois state line, ran north through Milwaukee, Sheboygan, Manitowoc, Kewaunee, Algoma, Forestville, Maplewood, and Sawyer to Sturgeon Bay, and continued along the Green Bay side of the peninsula to Ellison Bay. It was later extended to Gills Rock.

Nowadays, Route 17 has its origin in Merrill, from which it meanders north-northeast. It has been demoted from the heavy red line it once merited to a thin black line on the map. Route 17 now expires at the Michigan state line, eight miles east of Phelps, Wisconsin.

In happier days, to motorists braving the uncertainties of early automobile travel, Route 17 was a marvel of the age. Just follow the signs! No need to ask directions at gas stations (there were no gas stations out there until later). No more "Blue Book," that epic volume which advised you to turn right at the "red school house" and then to go three and three-tenths miles to a "large oak tree," and then go two miles and a half to a "red barn with a big silo" etc. etc. Route 17 made the Blue Book passe. But then Route 17 became a victim of other forces which retired it to limbo too.

The old Episcopal Church in Jacksonport is just south of the town proper, about half a mile inland on an untraveled road. There is only a modest wave in the shoreline to mark where Baileys Harbor leaves off and

Entering Sister Bay from the North   1919

Jacksonport begins, and Jacksonport has no sheltering arm of land to form a natural harbor. Nevertheless, the logging business once thrived there.

The skeletons of several docks provide evidence that many vessels docked at Jacksonport, and much timber was shipped from there, but that is all over now. With the demise of the lumber industry, the big schooners sailed away into limbo and Jacksonport seemed to retire onto itself. It waited for commercial fishermen to come, but they sought protected harbors. It waited for tourism, but that was a long wait ahead.

The snapshot from which the picture was painted was taken in 1915 on a lazy Sunday in August, right after church. To the left of the church, beyond the open gate, a picnic was being held beneath a grove of trees.

The picnickers had brought their own provisions, and there was little that the ladies of the church auxiliary could offer them except pitchers of heavy cream that was to be poured over wild raspberries that they had gathered for their visitors. The ladies auxiliary was a most cordial group, most hospitable, and they served wonderful food, though they apparently had never heard of either calories or cholesterol.

The church itself was old in 1915. The rector at that time might well have been the one who took charge of it when it was built, for he was old too. He has been gone for years, but the church still stands and is used during the summer months.

It used to be painted white, but, in later years, the color has been changed to brown, making it blend inconspicuously with the grove of trees which has grown up around it.

✜ ✜ ✜

The Episcopal Church at Jacksonport 1915

Door County's colors include the varied greens of trees and foliage, the blue and turquoise of the water, the glistening white of the stone beaches, and the golden white of the sand beaches. But all these vivid, lively colors are punctuated with shades of gray that range from silver to deep purple and red-brown. Most of the gray derives from white-pine boards which start out yellow and weather to gray.

Fish houses were erected of such pine boards, on or near the shores of the abounding bays, and there usually were several of these stark buildings in a cluster. They were protected on the water side by log cribs filled with rocks and by large stones forming breakwaters that opened on the protected side to let fish boats in to shelter. In most instances, there was a slip with two gabled, oblong shacks, one on either side. The fish boat would be tied up in the slip when not in use, where it was easy to load and unload. The shanties themselves were built partially on shore and partially on pilings that extended out over the water.

Skiff along the shore at Ellison Bay, 1923

Fish Boat at rest in a Door County Bay 1927

These fish-house clusters were functional structures, built because they were needed. Their decoration was left to Mother Nature, with her brushes of time and exposure. She weathered them into perfect harmony with the shoreline and landscape behind, and no one could have done it better. No one!

Chapter 4
Anthem

Back when the world was putting itself together, a great glacier gouged out the Great Lakes and created the Niagara Escarpment. An escarpment is a long, precipitous ridge, and in this case, one thinks of Niagara Falls, way over at the other end of the Great Lakes. The Door County Peninsula is molded from the same rock formation as the one over which the Niagara River flows.

The two ends of the formation appear quite different. At the eastern end, the Niagara River dug away and created the famous Falls, and the river is still working on the project. At our end, the formation is tipped so that it slips serenely under the waters of Lake Michigan on the eastern side of the peninsula, while on the other, western side, it stands high, watching nervously as Apollo puts the sun to rest each day. In this way, the Niagara formation gives the peninsula the form it has today. Green Bay was formed in the confusion of it all, and its water laps warily at the base of the limestone bluffs frowning down on it.

At first, the shore was not usable by anything but birds, but the blue-green waters gradually carried out the tedious labor of etching out bays where the rock was weakest and grinding the chunks of rock to stones and sand. However, along the bay-side shores, the grinding never quite reaches the sand stage; along the bay, bleached white stones of varying sizes make the beaches picturesque but rather hard on the feet, and, without sand, the water there retains its crystal clarity. If you demand sand, try the Lake Michigan side of the peninsula. There the low shoreline is studded with sentinel pines guarding several stretches of sweeping sandy beach.

One of the bluffs on the bay side resisted more effectively the rigors of smashing water, driving snow, and insidiously penetrating ice, and holds its head higher than the others. The "Big Bluff" stands serene, facing the northwest where most of the weather is conceived. It is permanent, yet it changes depending on where you are when you see it. It is remote, and to see it best you must be out on the water. It becomes more impressive, more dominating, as you approach it, and as you drag your hand in the deep blue-green water, you're almost in the shade of its towering tree-covered cliff before you can discern huge rocks on the bottom, ghostly in the depths, marking a ledge which drops off into deep water. Small-mouth bass lurk along this ledge, bass who were born mad and would put up a fight at the sight of a lure. When the great storms come, the Big Bluff takes the beating of the elements head-on; when they have run their course, it gazes benignly upon them as they withdraw to their Valhalla to lick their wounds.

There are, of course, other bluffs up and down the Green Bay shore, mostly low, all tree-covered, all lovely. There are even a few, like Eagle Bluff and Door Bluff, that seem to rival the Big Bluff, until you go out and really compare them. Coming around the western shore of Washington Island from the north, you see the Big Bluff as the high spot on the peninsula; from Chambers Island looking north, it is just as dominant as when seen from the western shore of Green Bay in the upper peninsula of Michigan.

The Big Bluff rises about 160 feet out of the water, nothing like the grandeur of a Norwegian fjord, but still with resemblance enough to attract the Norwegians who gravitated to Door County and settled there.

There was a legend that no one could climb the face of the Big Bluff, though that proved to be nonsense. Just about half-way up its western face there is a large cave that yawns over the bay. Birds and bats use it handily. Other animals have difficulty getting there and no reason to stay. However, across the mouth of the cave someone hung a handkerchief! It stayed there more than fifteen years, too long to assume that a single handkerchief dangled in the mouth of that cave through winter storms and summer rains for all that time. It must have been replaced, probably time and again, so it is untrue, then, that the Big Bluff cannot be scaled.

The Big Bluff at Ellison Bay

That handkerchief caused quite a stir in the village, but it was nothing compared to the events of another summer many years ago. The hardy group of vacationers who came this way each summer had heard a breath of bad news one winter, and, when they returned to Door County the following summer, they rushed to the beach to see if the rumor was true.

It was. Standing on the stony shore, they gazed in disbelief across the bay at the side of the Big Bluff. There, a great swath of virgin timber had been cut away. Starting from where the vertical cliff began its sweep away from the water to form Hoagsville, a strip some two hundred feet wide had been cleared.

First there was resentment, then anger, and finally sadness, and with the sadness came questions. What sort of people would do this thing? What could bring someone to do such damage, to order this scar cut across the face of something so beautiful?

The answer, of course, was money. "They" were trying to revive the logging business. It was said that "they" planned to strip the bluff of its timber and leave it stark and barren all the way to Sister Bay. But why then had "they" stopped? The timber was still there. It belonged to "them," but the project was discontinued. It left only that one great scar. Then the equipment shipped out and the matter charged up to experience.

If you study the navigational charts of this area, you will see that the water along the Big Bluff gets very deep, very quickly as you move away from the shore. At the location of the scar, the bottom drops to about sixty feet just a little way from shore. That would be no stumbling block, some said; just build the wharf parallel to the shore. Fairly large ships could come almost to where the shore begins. But this argument forgot the ice that flows around the Big Bluff and into the bay each winter, sweeping everything before it. The storms come out of the northwest directly onto *that* shore. Protecting a wharf there would require a breakwater of exceptional strength that would have to be sixty to a hundred feet deep!

Cedars and rocks below the bluff   1923

No wonder the Big Bluff appeared content, almost as though it had arranged it all along. You could almost feel it murmuring that now it could settle back and let the great scar heal. Or was that only the lapping of waves on the shore? And the scar did heal. There is no vestige of it left to sadden those who first hated to see it. In fact, most of those people have gone too, because it was a long time ago.

The Big Bluff continues to face up to the brash summer squalls and to the raging storms of spring and fall, and it accepts with dignity the rigors of frigid winter blizzards. Each year they come on, and each year they are sent back spent and listless, while the Bluff remains the same.

Back in the early part of the century, several families spent every summer on Ellison Bay. From their cottages and tents, the Big Bluff was visible through the trees. It became an old friend. From almost anywhere they happened to be, just a turn of the head would bring it into view. Subconsciously it might even have symbolized eternity.

The youngest boy in one of these families began to think of the Big Bluff as something more than a friend. It filled him with too much awe to be merely a friend, and an inanimate one at that. For example, if a storm came, everyone went inside, but the Big Bluff just stayed there and faced it. If things got scary, as they did when thunder and lightning and sheets of rain struck, or when he would be walking down a dark path without a lantern at night, he purposely recalled the Big Bluff — calm, serene, aloof from scary things. He knew it was out there, just as it always was, and he wasn't quite so scared as he might have been. And this was a private thing to this lad, a very private, personal thing. Of course, it didn't replace his mother, father, and brother, but the Big Bluff was there too, and he came to feel that they — mother, father, and brother — got strength from it too.

This same boy had learned about God in church, in Sunday school, and at home. He felt he knew God quite well and was friendly toward Him. But he had never seen God. He had no way of knowing what God looked like. A long time before, someone had told him that God was an old man with a flowing white beard and a kindly face, dressed in white robes, sitting on a throne and judging everything. The boy got the idea that this kindly old man had no time for anything except judging people, and since his God did a lot of things besides judge people, the picture of the old man didn't suffice. He was left wondering what his friendly, helpful God did look like.

Since the boy couldn't (as he now says) relate to the kindly old man and since he *could* relate to the Big Bluff, he found himself thinking that maybe God looks like the Big Bluff. This seemed very fitting, because, wherever he was, he could always see the Big Bluff in his mind's eye — strong, eternal, patient. Even when very young, this boy could differentiate between "looking like" and "being," and never got the two confused.

It is rather strange that, even when he was little, this boy never told anyone what he thought God looked like. Not his mother, not his father, not his brother — not anyone. It wasn't because he didn't want to, nor because he was afraid he might be teased about it or anything like that. He truly felt they didn't have to be told; they knew it anyway.

Another thing — when the boy rowed across the bay toward the Big Bluff, he would drift in slowly, because he wanted to hear the soft rhythmic lap of the waves against the shore when the day was clear and there was just a slight movement of air. Way up among the trees clinging to the Bluff, a myriad of sounds issued forth from birds or animals, but mostly birds. Like the colors in nature, these sounds never clashed; they were in harmony. Then there was that little movement of air we mentioned. How it stirred the water to make gentle little waves! But it also stirred the trees and the shrubs growing on the face of the bluff into becoming a backdrop for the other sounds — sounds of the water, of the birds.

It made the boy wonder, for if the Big Bluff looked as God might look, then the sounds might be like the sounds that God would hear. The sound of angels singing did not *have* to be man-made sounds. . . .

What then of the storms — the raging crescendos of the surf, the fury of the wind, the staccato slash of rain or sleet, the thump of moving ice? Wagner, Beethoven, and many other composers wrote music depicting storms, but they only imitated the sounds of storms. What the boy was thinking of was the real thing — gigantic hymns of praise and glory in nature itself.

Perhaps that could be the singing of the angels, or, to be consistent, perhaps that could sound *like* the singing of angels. Some angelic songs were soft and lullaby-like; others bore the triple forte of thunder and lightning in mighty tribute. The boy though it was quite possible — particularly if you thought the Big Bluff looked like God.

Speaking of what God looked like conjures up thoughts of the Greeks and Romans and their myriad Gods — a God for everything and for every situation. The Germanic and Scandinavian races had their share, too, including, among others, Wotan, chief of the Gods.

The early settlers in what came to be the Door County Peninsula were newly come from central Europe and from the Scandinavian countries. They yearned for the rocky cliffs of the Rhine River or of towering fjords. In a way, the high bluffs of the rocky shore of Green Bay reminded them of home. When they spied a large cave on the face of a bluff, they were tempted to imagine it with Lorelei, and they almost could hear the siren songs luring fishermen to their doom on the rocks below.

And then there was Death's Door — the passage between the head of the peninsula and Washington Island. It was deep and narrow, with unpredictable currents and strange gusts of wind that made it fraught with danger. Just the place for some of the fabled Rhinegold to be hidden there on a pinnacle of rock in the restless water, waiting for another Siegfreid to return what justly belonged to the Rhinemaidens.

The Big Bluff at Ellison Bay   1929

Of course, this was just a fantasy to help to pass the long winter nights. Except . . . every fisherman along those Green Bay shores had heard it — a strange thunder-like rumbling or muttering, usually on summer afternoons, coming from out of the north. Probably from thunderheads banked there, over Death's Door. But, if you wanted to continue the fantasy, that rumbling could be the distant voice of Wotan summoning his Valkyrie out of Valhalla to do his bidding. The Valkyrie were his daughters, and it was their duty to bring the legend to its proper conclusion by rescuing the Rhinegold and taking it back to the Rhine River. And, since they were supposed to people Valhalla with warriors slain in battle for the protection of Wotan and all the Gods in Valhalla, it would be just as well to bring some lost fishermen along too, for they were hearty, hardy men and would swell the ranks of the heroes.

Logically, this should end the fantasy — except for that muttering in the summer clouds up north there, over the Door! Could it be that the "saying" of fishermen in northern Door County at the beginning of the twentieth century — their expression "Thunder Over the Door" — referred to Wotan's voice? Calling the Valkyrie?

But enough digression. What God looks like doesn't matter. What does matter is that God is so prevalent and can be something different to everyone. That young boy in the early years of the twentieth century was satisfied with his idea. In prior years, the first settlers of that remote county in northeastern Wisconsin had their own ideas, as well as the Nordic myths they brought with them, to occupy their thoughts on those long winter nights.

Chapter 5
Moto

If you stop to think about it, change is not the dominating constant in Door County, motion is. Of course, from the perspective of geological ages or even of centuries, changes in Door County are evident. But not many of us still remember Door County as it was even as recently as 1900.

Consider Eagle Bluff, Washington Island, Europe Lake, Mink River, Big Ellison Bluff, or the polished round stones at Little Sister Bay, and yes, consider Death's Door — all always in motion. The water, the trees, the clouds in the sky, the winds — always in motion. Those are the things people experience; those are the things dominating our days and years.

Sometimes, on a clear day, thunder could be heard out of the north, and there used to be an expression among the commercial fishermen to describe it. They would say there was "thunder over the Door." Where the expression came from and where it went no one seems to know. The thunder is still to be heard, though few seem to take notice of it.

Perhaps thunder out of the north meant to our forebears that there were storms brewing, and brewing near Death's Door specifically. The French explorers had good reason to name the stretch of water between the end of the peninsula and Washington Island *Porte des Morts* ("door of the dead"), and proof of the accuracy of their judgement abounds in the numerous skeletal remains of sailing ships that littered the shore and bottom of the Door. All along the southern shore of Plum Island, wooden ribs of those old ships bleached in the sun, keels torn and cracked by the rocks and waves, masts splintered. The action of wind and water has now destroyed most traces of those unfortunate boats, but their legacy lives on in the name and memories of the place.

The entire passage between the top of the peninsula and Washington Island, the peninsula's crown, measures about five miles east to west and four miles from Northport to the shore of Washington Island proper. Strategically placed "plumb" in the center of this body of water is Plum Island. To its south, toward Northport, is *Porte des Morts*, Death's Door; to its north is Detroit Passage, too shallow for big maritime traffic, but offering more shelter for fishing boats and pleasure craft. Just off the southern shore of Washington Island, long slender Detroit Island forms and protects Detroit Harbor, home of numerous pleasure boats and headquarters for the ferries to Gills Rock and Northport. Out to the southeast of Plum Island, marking the entrance to Death's Door, is tiny Pilot Island, which used to house a lighthouse and crew when sailboats were in style. The lighthouse structure remains, but it is now unmanned. Shoals and reef-like islets dot the Lake Michigan side of the tip of the peninsula and the Detroit Passage waterway, but none of them infringe on the deep water of the *Porte des Morts* channel.

Around the turn of the century and before, *Porte des Morts* passage was extensively used by sailing vessels carrying cargoes in and out of the growing industrial towns of Green Bay, Escanaba, Marinette, and Menominee along the southern and western shores of Green Bay. Sailing ships moved back and forth between them and the various ports along Lake Michigan's eastern shore. It was too far to go around via Chicago by train, and, at that time, big trucks for long distance hauling hadn't even been invented. The Sturgeon Bay ship canal was too narrow for any type of shipping except propeller-driven craft, which were not then prevalent on upper Lake Michigan. Consequently, the shortest way from Lake Michigan to the lumber and fish from Green Bay was through Death's Door.

If the weather was clear, the passage ordinarily was without incident. Nasty storms could blow up in the summer, and, during the spring and fall, gales were particularly likely to brew in northern Lake Michigan and bear down on the *Porte des Morts* with furious intensity. When that happened, catastrophes often occurred. The ships' skeletons mentioned above — wooden bones of vessels which had sought passage and found disaster — were mute evidence of the perfidy lurking in the Door.

Porte des Morts from Northport

Once winds enter the Door, they become fickle. They change direction and pile new waves on top of those already established, but going in the other direction. Thus, a sailing ship might come into the Door on a northwest heading, spurred along by a specious north wind driving gray scudding clouds before it, then abruptly experience a wind shift, and, instead of bearing away from the rocky shore of Plum Island, find itself being blown onto the jagged rocks there, where relics on the shore bore witness to the looming calamity.

Porte des Morts

Plum Island Life Saving Station   1913

What causes the unrest in the winds besieging the Door? Why are the currents so capricious? Perhaps it is due to the placement of land masses, or to the relationships of water masses, or to variations in water temperatures. Perhaps the shallows that edge the deep channel of the Door have something to do with the behavior of currents and the movement of water between Lake Michigan and Green Bay. There are no tides in the lakes — at least none that are regular from day to day — but still the lure of the moon may have its effect. Sometimes the motion in Death's Door is gentle, sometimes restless, sometimes brisk, sometimes furious, but it's always there. Sometimes the motion results in the thunder of waves, or the thunder of wind, or Thunder Over the Door.

Of course, nowadays, most of the threat is removed. No sailing vessels now ply commercial routes around the Great Lakes. But it hasn't been so very long since they did. Back in 1912, the Door was still an uncertain quantity — not for freighters, which were powered by steam and kept their appointed courses regardless of the caprices of the Door — but for fishing boats and for a form of small cargo vessel called, naively, "hookers." The name was inspired not by pretty girls but by their similarity to certain small sailing craft used by the Dutch — clumsy, slow, and relatively safe craft from the Hook of Holland.

Once Apollo had driven his flaming chariot below the horizon of Green Bay, twilight was upon the land and another sort of light appeared. This was back before electricity had taken over and when gas was too dear and Door County too remote for it to be used extensively. Kerosene, or coal oil, as they used to call it, was the energy source for lighting. Wood was most often the energy source for heating and cooking, but kerosene lamps provided light, and there were many different kinds. Plain ones had a container for kerosene, a wick, and a glass chimney; fancy lamps had the same things, but there was also a decorative shade crowning the chimney or a reflector to diffuse and thereby enhance the light. The most glamorous

Ellison Bay cottage with an Aladdin lamp   1916

lamps were those with incombustible network hoods over the kerosene flame which gave off a brilliant light when they were heated to incandescence. The incombustible hoods were called mantles, and they were unbelievably fragile and amazingly bright. In fact, mantles were so effective that they were used with gas jets in the larger cities.

The only electricity available in upper Door County around the turn of the century came from batteries in flashlights. But flashlight batteries wore out rapidly or deteriorated because of exposure, and for years they were nowhere near as satisfactory as the tried and true kerosene lanterns.

At this time, trout were extremely abundant in Green Bay and Lake Michigan, and every morning except Saturday and Sunday, Emil Nelson, Charley Anderson, and Hilder Erickson (among many others) gathered their crews, started their engines, and cast off. Their destinations were the buoys bobbing about in the waters surrounding the peninsula, and it made little difference where they went, for there were trout everywhere. All day long the lines would be brought into the boats laden with fish. Once the fish were removed from the hooks, they were rebaited and reset below the surface to attract another day's catch.

Finally, when the sun had edged its way toward the horizon (if you were fishing on Green Bay) or impaled itself on the spires of pine and cedar (if your boat was positioned in Lake Michigan) the job was done, the lines would be cast off from the last buoy, the engine started, and everyone available began the work of cleaning the fish. This was feasting time for the ever-present gulls. They swooped and swarmed, grabbing every vestige of the fish entrails tossed over the side.

The gulls were (and still are) an automatic disposal system. They were sure, they were thorough, and they were easy. The gulls were always there from first to last of the cleaning process, performing their appointed task of keeping the ecology in balance.

Meanwhile the sun would become hidden, as Apollo crossed the finish line of another day. One of the crew would go forward to light the running lamps — red to port, green to starboard — and then hang one lantern above the pilot house and another, higher, aft of it. Two other lanterns dangled from hooks inside the cabin giving off an eerie light which danced uncertainly with the motion of the boat.

After a relatively calm day, twilight sometimes brings a cessation of any breezes that have been stirring, a sort of transition from the sweat of the day to the tranquility of the night. And, just as the running lights on a fish boat were lit, so also the stars would come out and the lights on shore appear, making beacons to mark the progress of the boat to her home mooring. Then, with the advent of night, some wayward breeze will find itself, slowly become agitated, and finally assertive, as it decides on a quadrant from which to blow. Gently, that is, not hard, for there are no strong winds on such nights.

Some of the boats would make their way from Lake Michigan through Death's Door to their home ports on Green Bay. But there was no alarm on nights when the Door was passive, and other craft might come with their burdens of fish from Green Bay back around to Baileys Harbor and Jacksonport on the Lake Michigan side. It seemed odd that they would reverse like that, but fishermen go to where they have had good luck and where their buoys stake out their claims. Others still don't transit the Door, but stay on their own sides, and they were just as happy and their rewards just as great.

One particular fisherman was coming back from Lake Michigan to his home port on the Green Bay side. Off to starboard now, over the green light, was the lighthouse on Pilot Island, only a flashing beam in the darkness. Up ahead, the Range Light marked Plum Island's position. To the left, over the red port light, the lamps of Gills Rock would soon become visible, once Table Bluff was left astern. The lights ashore seemed to be moving while the boat remained stationary in space, and the shush of her bow wave, the reflections of her running lights — red, green, and white — and an occasional monosyllable from the cabin formed her only links with the world of life and motion. Of course, the engine throbbed and the exhaust spoke out loud and clear, but the men on board only heard those sounds if they should change unaccountably.

Gills Rock was on the port beam now, but it quickly dropped astern and then was unceremoniously cut off by a protruding bluff. The shore lights were extinguished one by one. Soon all was darkness except the stars forming the canopy overhead. Their combined candlepower marked the tiny waves with quicksilver and threw the bluff into black relief. The soft breeze seemed like wind drift from a friendly star — little wonder that the fishermen sat back and let their minds dwell on fancy rather than fish.

Door Bluff loomed mountainous, but it was only an illusion amplified by the contrast of the glow from millions of stars and the deep shadows it spawned. Its hugeness tapered and evolved into a low shoreline where small waves were breaking, silver streaks that flashed and then dissolved into night again.

Far ahead and high up, a particularly bright speck of light came into view, as another low bluff swept by to port. "There's Mike's now, off to starboard there," someone said. That was Mike Anderson's Hillside Hotel, and the bright speck of light was the kerosene mantle lamp in the beer parlor.

Without seeming to, fancy fled and reality returned with the sighting of Mike's beer parlor. The three crew members stirred and began preparation for landing at the big dock. Lights appeared through the woods on shore, Emil Nelson's fish house was evident off to port, and the flicker of a lantern through the trees betrayed someone walking along the shore road.

A fish boat bringing its catch to the big dock 1928

One shadow began to etch itself out of the gloom ahead, and one very dim glow became a window and then another, while the night sky silhouetted a small building rising above the longer shadow of the approaching dock. As the boat nudged against the ancient logs and even older stones of the cribs of the big dock, figures materialized above to take the lines and make them fast to log posts.

"Good catch?" someone asked.

"Ya," came the answer from the deck.

With that the boxes of cleaned fish were swung aloft by those on board and caught by others waiting on the dock. One by one they were carried into the small, square building where Mike Anderson and his assistant carefully weighed the catch, box by box, then packed the fish in shipping boxes amid volumes of shaved ice and stacked them to one side. From time to time, the assistant would return to the big cakes of ice in their bin and shave off more ice — enough for the next box — with a tool made for the purpose.

"Yonder comes Emil," observed a man standing outside.

Another turned his ear to the breeze and concurred. "Ya, he's late."

It was a big night that night, but that's the way it was in those days. Erickson followed Nelson, and there were two more fishermen after that. But, finally, all the fish from all the boats were iced, packed in shipping boxes, sealed with boards nailed across the top, and stacked, ready for the next hooker or steamer to come by. Two hanging lanterns were snuffed out. Then, carrying a third, Mike Anderson and all interested bystanders made their way off the big dock, up the hard gravel road, and so to Charley Ruckert's General Store. They didn't stop to buy anything in particular, but to see and be seen, to talk and be talked to — usually in monosyllables — and that was enough.

The "Big Dock" in Ellison Bay   1915

The men who used to gather at Charley Ruckert's store were a brotherhood. They all worked hard at hard physical work. They all braved the hazards of the lake, the bay, and, of course, Death's Door. They all had good wives and sturdy children, and they all went to church. All of them cussed some, and usually for good reason. They all liked a good quaff of heady beer, and, to a man, they loved the life they led.

Mike Anderson had spent most of his adult life aboard sailing ships on the Great Lakes. During many of those years, he was master of the ships on which he sailed, but he finally gave up the sea and bought the Hillside Hotel (or Boarding House) from Charley Ruckert. He added the two-story structure shortly after he bought the property in 1902. Mrs. Anderson ran the Boarding House and, incidentally, her husband as well. Except, that is, when he repaired to the big dock and established himself in the fish house.

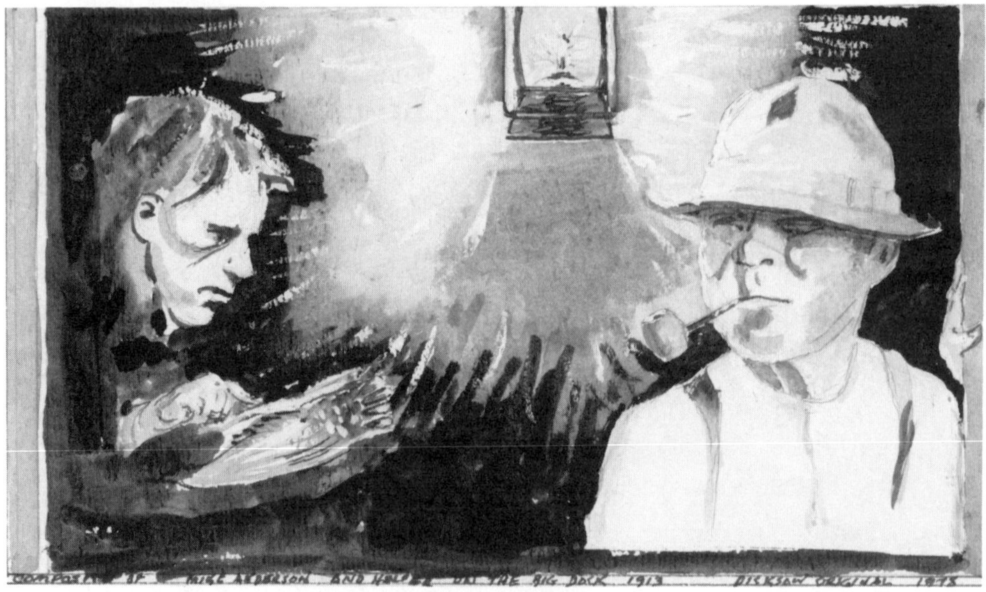

Mike Anderson & helper in the fish shanty on the big dock 1913

Captain Mike Anderson's Hillside Hotel 1912

Any day in spring, summer, or autumn, Mike Anderson would be off with the first sound reaching him from any incoming fish boat. Down the hill he would trudge toward the Big Dock, a trail of smoke from his corncob pipe swirling behind him.

Back up at the Hillside Hotel, as afternoon wore into evening and evening passed into night, one could watch the incoming boats, their lights eerily reflected in the ever-moving water. The hoarse voices of the fishermen and of the fish-house crew echoed across the water until the last boat was in, the last trout iced, and the last board nailed onto the last crate. Finally, when the lights went out in the fish house and the last boat was moored for the night, the crews plodded wearily over to the corner at Ruckert's store before separating to walk toward their various homes, where supper and bed awaited them.

After a brief stop and a word or two at Ruckert's store, Mike Anderson left, carrying nothing more than himself and a lantern; he plodded along the road and halfway up the hill to the hotel which bore his name but which his wife actually ran. She was a large, jovial woman, and it was said that she ruled Mike with an iron hand. But he didn't seem to mind, and everything worked out well. Besides, no one could cook the way Mrs. Anderson could — no one else's baked trout was so succulent, no one could match her pies dripping with goodness, and cherries.

But this night, Mike wanted a long drink of keg beer before he went in for the supper he knew his missus would have ready for him. It had been a long day for Mike, with a lot of lifting, a lot of pushing, and a lot of fish. As he pulled open the door of his beer parlor, the sudden blaze of mantle-amplified kerosene light dazed him, and he pulled his hat lower on his brow. Somehow he preferred the somber light of a fish-stained lantern to this bright evidence of progress. As he closed the door on the darkness outside, he heard the last fish boat cut her engine, and he knew that all the boats were in and tied up. So he had his beer and went in to supper.

Garrett bay with Gills Rock beyond   1921

The beer parlor's lights may have been the most sharply brilliant, but the most elegantly lighted of all the local establishments was Charley Ruckert's General Store. He used the same mantle kerosene lamps, but he had more of them than anyone else, and he did not turn them up as high, so the light was diffused, softer, and more pleasant.

Ruckert's store is still there, looking much the same as it did in 1912, but the name has changed, and it is now called the Pioneer Store. Be that as it may, it operated as Charley Ruckert's General Store for nearly seventy-five years, and, though the name is changed, the building goes on and on, like the Big Bluff, the Door, and the passing seasons. Everything from high-button shoes to flour, from piece goods to coal oil, and from store-bought cookies and crackers to horse feed, including canned goods, candy, hay, and salt meat, was sold in Ruckert's store. Charley Ruckert had installed stools before the two counters, one on either side of the store, where customers could sit while contemplating their purchases or catching their breath. Horse collars and hats hung from the ceiling, and there was a huge wood stove right in the middle of it all. From opening to closing, there were people in the store to buy, to talk, and to trade. And Charley Ruckert was there, a very large man with an equally large smile, a flowing mustache, and a welcome for those he knew — and he knew everyone. Or, if he didn't, he soon would.

Charley Ruckert — Proprietor

Ruckert's Store 1900-1920

But it didn't really matter which particular bay this was, with one hotel halfway up the hill and the other in town, with a big dock that had two red buildings on it, with a church whose steeple marked the center of the village, and with a blacksmith shop right across the way. You could go into almost any bay on the peninsula and find almost the same thing. The bluffs might be higher or lower, or there might be no bluff at all. The bay might be wider or deeper, and perhaps the docks would be longer logging docks or shorter fishing docks, but you'd always find a Mike Anderson, a Charley Ruckert, and an Emil Nelson, or their local counterparts.

The soul of Door County was really reflected in its lights, from the lowly lanterns with their infinite uses, to the new, modern Aladdin lamps with their kerosene mantles that were so fragile and brilliant. Yes, there were also the stars which shone on the gently waving trees and undulant water on summer nights (and on the billowing snow and frozen bays in winter), and even the inimitable Milky Way was overshadowed by the moon when it was out now and then. But, despite this splendor, the coal-oil lamps remained evident until someone put them out.

Sometimes, people didn't put them out. Some cottagers, up from the city for the summer, were a bit apprehensive in the deep night of the woods, and they would leave a lantern dimly lit as a night-light. One might almost accuse them of taking too literally the litany about "ghosties and things that go bump in the night." Alas, most of the things that went bump in the night were porcupines looking for a way to satisfy their craving for salt, and as for ghosties, you can't have everything, even in the deep woods at night. It's strange that these cottagers couldn't recognize a porcupine by its sound; let them hear the "put-put-put" of a fish boat coming around the bluff, and they could name the boat every time.

It was all so serene — the sky, the water, the summer nights. No tympani, no brazen brass, just the muted sweep of violins, the plaintive notes of an English Horn, and the soft cry of cellos. This is how it was most of the time in Door County, and in the Door.

❖ ❖ ❖

Anybody going to Garrett Bay usually went on foot or behind a good team of horses because the road there was suspect at best. Once there, most folks took a quick look and went on to Gills Rock. But Mrs. Ella Dana, a native of the area, did more; she built a summer resort on Garrett Bay.

The Garrett Bay Inn 1919

Until that time there was nothing like it north of Ephraim — boarding and lodging hotels, yes; resort hotels, no — and the new Garrett Bay Inn was indeed a summer resort. It had a sunny lobby with comfortable chairs and couches, and a huge stone fireplace. A game room also had a fireplace, and the dining room was as bright and attractive as the food Mrs. Dana served. You couldn't find better sleeping rooms north of Milwaukee, and the fact that the plumbing was inside raised eyebrows even in Ephraim and Fish Creek. The Garrett Bay Inn is shown as it appeared in 1919.

The Inn had a boat dock and breakwater, a strip of sandy beach, and two tennis courts. Pitching quoits was surprisingly popular. In the woods just up the shore, Mrs. Dana built a few cottages for guests who preferred to be away from it all, though the cottages had no cooking facilities.

The Inn was a great success and prospered for several years until a fire started there one winter and left the Garrett Bay Inn a smoldering ruin. However, Mrs. Dana was undaunted and soon thereafter replaced the first floor of the Inn — that is, the part including the lobby, game room, and dining facilities — and added several cottages. Again she prospered and continued to do so for many years. But then came another winter and another fire. At long last, Mrs. Dana had had it, but she and her fine resort were highlights of the first quarter of this century in Door County.

Many of the early outlanders vacationing in upper Door County spent whole summers in tents, often two or more, supplemented by a more substantially built privy. One tent was used for living and one (or more) for sleeping. If it rained, a big log fire was built outside the living tent, while novels and cards and games were available inside. Or you could go fishing. When it was clear, you never stayed in the tent.

Several things were associated with tent living. One was the hand pump. It took a little work to get the crystal-clear water up from where it lurked in the rock below, and one had to carry pails filled to the brim from the well back into the house. But, once tasted, the water was worth the effort. This was hard water, *very* hard water. Rainwater was soft, but it too had to be carried inside by the pailful. In those wonderful days, there was no running water in rural Door County except what ran off the roof into a cistern.

The new pump 1915

Summer quarters on Ellison Bay   1915

Whether water came from a rain barrel, from a cistern huddled beneath the eaves, or from a pump, it eventually found its way into large porcelain pitchers which rested fat-bellied and wide-lipped in broad matching porcelain washbasins. Of course, not all were made of porcelain, and they did not all match — some were of enamelled metal that rapidly acquired nicks and bruises where rust prospered. Outlanders seemed to favor enamelled metal equipment, but they soon did away with the pitchers and went directly from a water pail to the basin, via a dipper.

Then too there was a third porcelain item; it was round and pot-shaped and, in fact, took its name from its shape. The potty lingered under the bed and was put to use when it was too far to the outdoor privy or just too darn cold. These porcelain pieces are now genuine antiques, though our parents and grandparents thought of them as modern conveniences and would have been indignant had they foreseen their use as flowerpots.

Cooking was done on a kerosene stove vented out the back of the tent, and there was an oven that could be placed atop one of the burners. Perch and bass were fried deliciously. Trout was baked to perfection. Of course, there were many other things to eat besides fish, and, in the outdoors, they were good eating too.

The sleeping tent was much like the living tent, except that tables and chair and the like were replaced by beds, and one was careful to tie the tent flaps on the inside, lest some curious porcupine or, heaven forbid, a skunk came calling. Sleeping in a tent was much like spending the night in the open, except that it did not rain in your face unless the tent leaked. That was why a spread of canvas over the tent was used. It was called a "fly" and proved very effective.

The night sounds of the forest, the water, and the animals proved not to be scary, for they blended into your dreams so naturally that you missed them when they had to be exchanged for the cacophony of city sounds. And it is a fact that the porcupines and skunks were most considerate.

An early "facility" in northern Door County 1914

Deep in many a patch of sylvan greenery rose a privy, with sunlight glinting through a canopy of leaves and casting intricate, moving shadows all about. Privies were not the multipurpose chambers that modern bathrooms are, but they had an indispensable place in society in rural Door County at the beginning of this century. Outlanders, up north for the summer, often made sure that their privies were secluded in sylvan greenery so that the sun would glint through surrounding leaves, providing it wasn't raining. But, to year-round residents, a privy was simply an outbuilding of necessity. If ever there was any glamor attached to them, it was dispelled apace in inclement weather, especially in winter. Outdoor privies had their day while we were growing up on the peninsula, in sun and in shade, and they must be included in any factual account of those times.

Chapter 6
Adagio

Since you have to lay railroad tracks and build roads before you can use them, pioneers have always turned first to water transportation. Early in this century, there not only were no really good roads, there were no modern trucks to run on them. Railroad tracks had formed a network across the whole country by that time, though there were none north of Sturgeon Bay. There *still* are none north of Sturgeon Bay, and it's safe to say that there never will be. But there was produce to be moved out of Door County, and sailing ships had to do the job, carrying mostly lumber and fish.

As areas were cleared of their trees, little villages appeared. Their houses and buildings and churches were clustered near docks that projected out into the clear blue-green water and to which boats tied up. Some of the buildings were stores. Stores need merchandise, and some of it had to be brought in from outside the peninsula — and that had to be by boat.

To serve this need, "hookers" were created. Regular sailing vessels were too much involved with lumber and fish to bother with package freight for the local stores. Considering modern nomenclature, it is only prudent to reiterate the derivation of the name hooker, lest we leave those proud old boats with a stigma on their good names; they were called after similar small vessels that plied the waters off the Hook of Holland's coast.

Hookers ranged in length from about forty to perhaps seventy feet. They were wide of beam, and, early on, they usually affected two masts, fore and main. They were staunch and slow and carried anything that needed to be moved, even lumber if the lumber schooners were running behind. They were not pretty as such, but they were picturesque.

Although no one realized it to begin with, hookers came to represent the transition from sail-powered to propeller-driven boats. At first hookers were driven by the wind alone, but then Kahlenburg and Straubel began turning out gasoline engines — primitive, ponderous, powerful, and, most important, very reliable. At first they were used as a supplement to sail, an auxiliary power source that could help a hooker get up to a dock when the wind was uncooperative or unpredictable.

The shift from sail to engine power was a slow one, but even the most "stand-pat" sailor of the day became enamored with the convenience of an engine with its attendant driving force, the propeller. Many hookers retained mainmasts and sails to fit them, but both masts and sails quickly became standby equipment used only in cases of dire emergency.   After a

A hooker with a cargo of trout   1910

A hooker nearing Ephraim dock   1913

time, the sails seemed so complicated and tedious that they were left on shore — to make more space for cargo, it was said. The last of the old hookers even had her mast unshipped, and thus, in at least that one case, the transition was complete.

Although they have long since been replaced — first by steamers, and latterly by trucks — hookers rendered an indispensable service all up Green Bay and along the north shore of Lake Michigan to Mackinaw City and Manitoulin Island. They quickly took over the job of moving fish to market, bringing sleek white salmon trout and whitefish which abounded in the waters of the area to Booth fisheries in Green Bay. They made many stops along the peninsula from Sturgeon Bay north to Egg Harbor, Sister Bay, Ellison Bay, Gills Rock, and Washington Island, and down the lake side to Newport, Rowleys Bay, Sand Bay, Appleport, Baileys Harbor, and Jacksonport. Earlier, hookers also made port at Ephraim and Fish Creek.

Hookers had their problems with *Porte Des Morts'* treacherous ways, but the addition of big Straubels or Kahlenburgs materially reduced the hazards along the way. Although hookers never ran on specific schedules, their arrivals were frequent enough so that one or another of them could be just around the point at any given time.

Another factor in the adagio pace of those times was the mail boat. Walter Olson's got the mail from Sturgeon Bay as far north as Ellison Bay regularly, six days a week. But farther north still was Washington Island, completely surrounded by water and separated from the peninsula by Death's Door, truly a challenge to the motto "The Mail Must Go Through."

The mail boat left Ellison Bay in the early morning for Washington Island, where the inbound mail was taken to the post office. After going home for noon dinner, the mailman returned to the post office, picked up the outbound mail, and made his way back to the mail boat tied up in

The "little bluff" and the "big dock" at Ellison Bay   1917

Detroit Harbor. From there he transported it by sea and by land to the Ellison Bay post office, where Walter Olson picked it up the next morning and carried it to Sturgeon Bay aboard his bus, or in winter, his sled.

Walter Olson's "mail coach" on the ice, Egg Harbor   ca. 1910

During the summer, this procedure was as near being pleasant as anything could be, though spring and fall offered equinoctial tantrums, and these tantrums could be hazardous. But winter was something else. At that time, Ellison Bay, the Green Bay shore above Ellison Bay, and Death's Door itself frequently froze to a depth of two or three feet. Under those circumstances, the mail was transferred by horse-drawn sled from Gills Rock. Unexpected thaws some-times occurred, and the ice floe itself tended to move, both of which could cause a bad case of the "willies" in even the most stout-hearted mailman.

In 1912 the mailman was Armour Kincaid — a fine man, a gentleman in every respect, and a good mailman. But finally, about 1914 or 1915, Armour Kincaid decided that he had had as much of the Door's frivolous attitude as he wanted. He applied for a transfer and turned the reins over to Captain Pete Anderson. The *E.H. Clayton*, which had been Kincaid's mail boat, was retired from government service and was replaced by the *Volunteer*, a larger, more powerful boat with a big, husky, two-cylinder Kahlenburg engine. She was indeed an intrepid craft, and her captain, Pete Anderson, was fearless. Together they made a most imposing and efficient team.

There were a few hardy vacationers in the northern peninsula who had forsaken both Ed Disgarden's Hotel in Ellison Bay and Mike Anderson's Hillside Hotel on the hill above town. They either had built their own basic cottages or were relying on tents. These cottagers maintained contact with the two hotels by taking their dinners at noon at one or the other.

One day, some of these hardier types boarded Pete Anderson's *Volunteer* for an outing to "the Island." It was a clear, calm day as the *Volunteer* made her way north past one low bluff and then a bigger one, Door Bluff. Later, with Table Bluff off the starboard bow, the *Volunteer* cleared into Death's Door. Off the starboard stern were Garrett Bay, then undeveloped, and Gills Rock, a thriving fishing village. To the right was the passage to Lake Michigan, a stretch of clear blue water as calm and peaceful as you could want that day, lazy even. The swells were long and gentle, left over from some blow now long gone.

The *Volunteer* stopped on the south shore of Plum Island, where passengers disembarked to view the views with eye and camera. Way out in Lake Michigan was little Pilot Island, its lighthouse standing sparkling white in the morning sun. The carefree group wandered along a path lined by tall oak trees, with pine, cedar, and sumac clustering beneath them, and the lacy branches of the trees danced rhythmically in a freshening breeze. Then the north shore and the life-saving station situated there opened before them, and they forgot that freshening breeze. Captain Anderson met the hikers at the Coast Guard station, where they came back aboard once more for the short trip across the passage to Detroit Harbor and dinner.

Everyone went to an inn owned by Ida and Bo. You guessed it, they were Andersons too, and the Idabo Inn boasted a thoroughly satisfactory dining room right down to the crisp pineapple fritters and lemon meringue pie. No one could gainsay those fritters or that pie, least of all the young boys, and parents were generous with their permissions, even though it might mean Phenolax later on.

When the party gathered dockside, gorged and sated, they found Pete Anderson with an eye cocked toward the northwest. He observed that "we might find a little weather in the Door." There was weather in the Door indeed!

As the *Volunteer* cleared the lee of Plum Island, the sea was already running, and the first wave took her brutally and without warning on the port bow. Up she went . . . SMASH . . . then into the next wave . . . WHAM . . . then into the next . . . and on and on. With several apprehensive passengers on board, you might think that Captain Anderson would have sought a way out, like turning back. Not he! He drove the *Volunteer* from one big wave to another, spray flying and green water crashing aboard over the lunging bow.

Mail boat *Volunteer* off Door Bluff   1921

This was bad enough, but, once clear of Plum Island, Captain Anderson was compelled to alter his course further to starboard, and this brought his craft into the trough of the waves. The pounding of the bow against the water was eliminated, but the roller-coaster ride from side to side was much more unnerving to most of the stomachs aboard than the smashing waves had been. One of the four young boys in the group was seasick; another was scared stiff. The last two amused themselves by leaning out of the hatch on the lee side to see how deep into the water they could plunge their arms with each roll. Pete Anderson was quite entertained by their game, but no one else happened to see them.

The *Volunteer* rolled crisply and cleanly in a cross sea, and she handled herself with contempt for the waves that were scaring many of the passengers nearly out of their wits. She came down from each crest with a flourish and then readied herself for the next one. Her master appeared slightly bored with the whole thing, except for the two boys who kept him amused.

Once in the lee of Table Bluff, the seas rapidly abated, but it was not calm except in relation to what it had been. Now an adjustment in course brought the waves onto the *Volunteer*'s stern, and they carried her along ahead of them like a surfer on a board.

Later that evening, still painfully aware of their afternoon's experience, the group walked down to the big dock where the *Volunteer* was tied up. Once on land, their digestive tracts had stopped churning, and they had just enjoyed supper at Disgarden's Hotel. Pete Anderson was sitting on the fantail of his craft, eating lamb sandwiches he had brought from home and reading day-before-yesterday's newspaper. Every now and then he scooped water out of the bay with a long-handled dipper to enjoy a cool drink. It was then he told the group about the boys dipping their arms into the waves on the way across. He thought it was funny, but one of the mothers nearly fainted.

There once was a hooker named *Lucille*. In her early days, she was a beauty as hookers go — sleek, slim, and graceful — she had a tall mast and a vast billowing sail. In fact, she had two sails — the other was a slender triangle of white canvas that swept from the masthead to the end of the long, proud bowsprit. She was handsomely painted — dark green below

The old hooker *Lucille* with the mail boat *E.H. Clayton* just aft   1914

and glistening white above. *Lucille* was the Belle of the Bay. She was one of the original hookers and, therefore, one of the first to grow old. When they sawed off her aristocratic bowsprit, she gained a new, heavy-duty, three-cylinder, Straubel gasoline engine, so that really wasn't so bad, for it made her even more maneuverable.

Later, her mighty mast was sacrificed, the better to fill her hold with fish and pine planks. At the end, the steamers *Bon Ami*, *Sailor Boy* and *Thistle*, now confining their activity to Green Bay alone, took away her trade. That is, they did when they could keep the *Thistle* afloat. The *Lucille* was a pretty little ship, but she was very old and very, very tired, and her bilge pumps worked feverishly whenever she was out. Finally, *Lucille* was retired and simply took up dock space at Gills Rock.

One day, an ambitious young man bought her. He fixed her up as best he could, put on some brave new coats of paint and tuned up her three-cylinder engine. He extended her cabin forward to within ten or twelve feet of the bow. Below, benches were placed where fish boxes had once been stored. The fish were gone, as were the boxes that had held them, but *Lucille* was never — *never* — to get rid of the aroma they left. He then put *Lucille* up for hire!

A year or two after their experience with Pete Anderson and the *Volunteer*, the same group of cottagers, perhaps with a few additions and deletions, chartered the *Lucille* for an outing to Washington Island. This time the Door behaved itself, and all was well. Some of the passengers credited their smooth journey to the size of the *Lucille*, but that wasn't it at all. The Door that day was simply placid, proving (to some) that everything said about it wasn't true at all. In fact, some of the passengers therewith chartered her for a trip to Marinette, where they could catch the Chicago Northwestern train home.

It was early September when they set out for Marinette on their homeward voyage. *Lucille* was well-stocked with gasoline, and she carried an extra gallon-can of oil (just to be on the safe side). The group of passengers established themselves on the forward and after decks with small folding chairs and parasols. It was a gala party as they passed the Big Bluff and started out across Green Bay.

For no reason, really, Captain Mike Anderson was invited to go along on this trip. He was, of course, an old and proven lake skipper, while her owner was not. Anyway, he came along.

In the beginning it was quite a lot of fun, but gradually the parasols came down, for the wind was getting crisp, and clouds were covering the sun. Then the clouds in the northwest got deeper in color — much deeper, almost purple — and the wind became angry. The passengers now had a choice; they could remain on deck and get soaked with splashes of rain and the spray from the mounting seas, or they could go down into the security of the cabin and enjoy the fumes from the engine blended with the ancient odor of long-deceased fish.

As time went on, the driving waves pushed the sluggish hooker about, and Captain Anderson took over the helm. He found the old boat unresponsive and floundering, but he was able to coax her along until he made the shelter of Chambers Island and took the stress off her. Then, with the island between her and the storm, old *Lucille* sort of got her feet under her and, in spite of the beating she had taken, once more set about getting to where she was supposed to go.

Captain Anderson was openly concerned. *Lucille* was carrying a great deal more water in her bilge than she was supposed to, and, with each wave, the water would slosh to one side with a rush, making it doubly hard for her to recover. To add to the problem, the wash back and forth was amplifying the rolling, and, once clear of Chambers Island again, the full brunt of the storm would be back on the old craft. But she made it. After a little more buffeting, Mike Anderson was able to turn her bow away from the charging seas and let them carry her down to Marinette.

Once within the breakwater and made fast to the dock, the shaken passengers said their farewells and made their way up to the train station. Trains running on rails attached to solid ground had a great appeal just then, it seems.

Meanwhile Mike and her owner took *Lucille* two or three hundred yards up the harbor and beached her. She had two boards loose and a split in her starboard bow, both below the water line. It had been touch and go! They were able to repair her sufficiently to get her back to Gills Rock where, eventually, she rotted away.

Thus ended the story of an old and once-happy hooker!

✠ ✠ ✠

Porte des Morts enraged was an awesome thing — the percussion section of nature's orchestra, joined by the full brass. If you were safe behind stout doors and walls and windows, it was a thing of shocking beauty — something to be marveled at. But, if you were out in it on the water, it became simply awesome! A place where prayers were said and one's life passed before bloodshot eyes one last time. Maybe storms don't actually brew in that space between the head of the Door County peninsula and Washington Island, thence to go storming up, down, or across Green Bay. But, if you are once caught in the cross-seas spawned in the Door, you might well wonder.

You might also form an opinion about whether there really is Thunder Over The Door.

Chapter 7
Finale

Transportation! That business of getting from here to there. During the early days of the twentieth century, automobiles were scarce, and at that time they were not particularly comfortable nor were they what you could call dependable. At least, they were not as dependable then as they are in the latter part of the century. Garages with able mechanics were an exception. In the cities, if a man was adept with cars he usually opened his own shop and did work by appointment, and he was likely to become a very busy man. Not rich, but busy!

But that was in the cities. Out in the countryside, someone acquainted with cars and handy at fixing them was hard to find. If trouble occurred, a blacksmith was the man of last (and sometimes only) resort. It was not unusual for a stranded motorist to approach a blacksmith with his problem and then to have the blacksmith leave his forge and approach the offending vehicle, hammer in hand. Perhaps the automobile didn't actually cringe as blacksmith and hammer approached, but motorists often did, and they often had second thoughts about stopping at a smithy for help.

Another matter to consider in those days was gasoline, and, especially, where to get it. There was not a gas station on every corner then, and you might have to go fifty miles or more between sources. And, after you came to a town where gasoline was supposed to be available, you had to find out who had it. Usually a store like Ruckert's had a small tank, but, all too frequently, it turned out to be empty.

Early in the century, Helmer Bergman opened a garage in Door County. Bergman was not just an able mechanic, he was an artist, for not all artists work in oils, pen and ink, or charcoal. Helmer Bergman was an artist who worked in iron. His wrought-iron creations became famous and are still in use in some of the older cottages in the peninsula, as well as in a lot of homes in Madison, Milwaukee, and Chicago.

During the winter, Helmer occupied himself with forge, hammer, and other tools, as he converted strips of iron about a half-inch square into wondrous wrought-iron railings, grills, decorative items, and fireplace sets. Some were on order to be delivered the next summer. Others were the artist's fancy of the moment.

As time went on, Helmer gradually turned the garage work over to his assistant, and then he sold that portion of his business, keeping the forge and his workshop in the back of the building. There, in his private domain, he continued the work he loved so much and at which he was so good.

Quite some time before Bergman gave up repairing automobiles, he created a masterpiece from a small evaporated-milk can and some hot solder. Although it was, in fact, only a small thing, it was a graphic example of his ingenuity. One day when two cars scraped together on a very muddy road, the larger of the two had had a hubcap torn off. It is rather startling to consider that two cars had got that close together, considering that there were very few cars and a great deal of space. Nevertheless, it happened, and the hubcap — in that era a functional rather than decorative device — was irreparably torn and twisted. Without it, the grease from the axle would leak out, causing further damage, and at that time spare parts were usually no nearer than Milwaukee, which proved to be the case in this instance. Thus, the car was immobilized for at least a week.

Then Helmer improvised. In that day and time, you could usually find an empty evaporated-milk can on any trash pile. Helmer found one. The fit over the nub of the axle was a little loose, but passable. Smearing hot solder around the inside of the can and then quickly screwing it onto the threaded nub was the work of but a minute. Result? Screwing on the solder formed new threads, and the car had a hub cap — one that served its needs for the *two* weeks it took to get another sent up from Milwaukee. Of course, such a thing couldn't happen now — considering present-day hubcaps — but, if it could happen, Helmer would have found a way to fix it.

✤ ✤ ✤

Driving up to Door county from Chicago or Milwaukee or Madison (or anywhere else) then was a challenge of major proportions. You could depend on the trip taking at least two days from Chicago — if everything went well — but you could never tell when something strange would happen to the unsuspecting and unprepared tourist.

In those wonderful days, tires and their inner tubes were mounted on steel rims that had flanges raised up around the inside and outside to hold the tire on. The wheels were permanently attached to the axle housing. In case of a flat tire, you changed the tire (on its rim) and not the wheel. There were permanent "stops" on the inside of the wheels to keep the rims from moving in, but, on the outside, lugs were screwed onto threaded bolts protruding from the wheel. Once the lugs were in place, it was to be assumed that everything was secure. But was it?

Imagine one passenger's reaction at seeing one of the tires quietly, fficiently, and steadily working its way off the wheel. Everyone else in the car was looking for the red schoolhouse on the right, just after the farm with the double silo, at which point they were to turn left. First, it was required to get word to the driver without causing panic among the other passengers. Then, once stopped, to get out the jack and lift the car before the wheel actually did come off.

The problem, they found, was that the lugs had worn smooth, permitting the rims to ease toward the outside, since they could not go in. The next town, according to the Blue Book Road Atlas, was ten miles.

"Watch it, Buster!" the driver said. So Buster watched it. Four times they had to stop to jack up the car and try to coax the lugs into holding just a little longer before reaching the next town. What if there were no lugs in the next town? But there were! Racine was the next town (heavens, are we only that far along?) and a brand new set of bulging lugs were secured.

If, by chance, you happened to break an axle — and that was not uncommon — it was paramount that you be near a large town where you could get a new one (or a new car). Failing that, you had to be somewhere where you could reach Helmer Bergman or someone like him!

But, it was a simple matter to get hooked on cars. Once you had had the convenience of having your car up on the peninsula, you forsook the conventional trains and steamships for the adventures and hazards of early automobile travel. Before that time, the trains and steamships thrived, and there were, of course, no airplanes.

The virtues of steamship travel from Chicago and Milwaukee to northern Door County have already been extolled, but not everyone going to Door County was fortunate enough to live close enough to Lake Michigan to take advantage of that means of transportation. And, there were also times when the ships didn't sail at the time you needed them, whereas the trains ran every day. The *S.S. Carolina* did her best to meet the demands placed upon her, and she was joined at times by the *S.S. Arizona*, the *S.S. Indiana*, or, infrequently, the *S.S. Georgia*.

It was always easy to recognize the *Georgia* when you saw her because she carried long arched steel braces that resembled the span of a bridge across a not-too-large stream. There was one on either side of the ship, implying, it seemed, that should the braces be taken away, the ship might come apart. They certainly were a strengthening device, though in reality the added strength probably wasn't needed and the braces' major function was as an aid to identification. But that was overkill; the red smokestack and chimed whistle were more than sufficient to allow quick identification of the ship, and you can't hear a steel brace nearly as well as you can a whistle. The braces are easily seen in the illustration on page 91.

Goodrich Steamer *Georgia,* at Sister Bay 1914

S.S. Indiana at Ephraim 1921

The Goodrich steamer *S.S. Arizona* approaching Sister Bay dock   1916

Some ships are thought "lucky" by the men who know them, and both the *Georgia* and the *Indiana* were regarded that way. Except for the braces that made the *Georgia* so distinctive, they were similar in profile, though the *Indiana* was a little longer and had greater displacement. Both served the Green Bay run long and well, and both were lengthened by some twenty-five feet at the Manitowoc shipyards during their years of service.

But, most vacationers preferred to leave upper Door county around the weekend, at which time the steamers were all bound for lower Michigan, where they could expect heavy shipments of fruit and vegetables as well as passengers. In late summer, the volume of business from Michigan was very attractive. That left the railroads. To be exact, that left the Chicago and Northwestern Railroad, though the closest it came to the Door County peninsula was Green Bay. Or was it? If you chartered a boat such as the hooker *Lucille* or wanted to take your chances on the irregular schedules of the steamers *Bon Ami* and *Sailor Boy*, you could sail across Green Bay to Marinette and take the train there.

Still there was another way at that time. The Green Bay and Western Railroad had affiliated lines running east and north from Green Bay. The Kewaunee, Green Bay and Western Railroad carried freight and a few passengers to Luxembourg and Kewaunee. The Ahnapee and Western Railroad carried mostly freight and a few passengers from Casco Junction to Algoma, Forestville, Maplewood, Sawyer, and Sturgeon Bay.

The combination of railroads making up the eastern end of the run carried passenger coaches on two trains between Green Bay and Sturgeon Bay. These passenger cars were anything but plush, but, as the summer population began slowly to increase, they came to be used more and more.

Passengers came down from the north under rather spartan conditions, riding in Walter Olson's stage. Upon arriving in Sturgeon Bay, the stage stopped first at the old Union Hotel near the railroad station, before proceeding to the post office and the station. The hotel was not

First "stage" of the trip home   1925

known for either comforts or cuisine, but it was definitely clean and most certainly respectable. After dinner, the travelers walked down to the railroad station, where they found their baggage on the platform. They then boarded the ancient day coach with its plush-covered bench seats.

After four hours aboard the stage, they were ready for a little luxury, but the seats had been built for utility rather than comfort, and, over the years, had proven to be utilitarian and nothing more. Besides, the railroad bed was designed for handling freight cars, and it is a fact that cows could be carried to the stockyards in Green Bay quite well — hogs too, for that matter — without undue complaint. But humans found the utilitarian bench seats a little much, particularly after a four-hour ride on the stage. True, if you were going only as far as Forestville, or from Maplewood to Algoma, and hadn't had a long bus ride, the seats might be acceptable, but they certainly were not luxurious or even comfortable. This problem must have come to the attention of some compassionate person at railroad headquarters, and an idea was born — the Door County Special!

One of the passenger cars was pulled off the line and sent to the railroad's shops where it was disemboweled and its back end was removed. Then it was painted and completely refurbished. New carpeting was installed, along with *cushioned* plush seats which pivoted to afford a view in all directions through the enlarged windows, and a new back platform was added. The Door County Special was ready for the road!

The back platform, which had replaced the old vestibule, was the most popular feature of the coach. Children loved to huddle on its tiny camp stools and be dusted with the cinders from the engine, several cars ahead. There is a certain acrid smell of cinders which reeks of railroading, and what little boy or girl didn't love it? From the parents' standpoint, the children and their clothes could always be washed, and the attractive back platform was in plain view, so that any brash actions on the part of the children could be quashed before they became dangerous. And for the children, it was great. If the train stopped in a field, they could safely lean out to determine whether there really was a cow on the track or if the stop was to pick up a neighbor. It was that kind of train. It was that kind of railroad line.

Door County Special at Sturgeon Bay   1913

The biggest thrill on the trip was when the Door County Special stopped in Casco Junction and then backed — yes *backed* — into Kewaunee. The brakeman would take his position of command at the very back of the platform. There he would handle the air pet-cock which, when opened, sent signals shrieking through the afternoon's calm to the engineer at the other end. These orders pierced out for the whole world to hear and for the engineer to obey unconditionally. They made the brakeman King-Emperor, Lord of all he surveyed, at least for the few minutes it took the train to back into Kewaunee. All the children were delighted to be part of it, and, when the brakeman unbent sufficiently to explain what he was doing, it became the highlight of the trip.

Kewaunee sometimes presented an additional thrill for the younger set. The Kewaunee railroad station was within sight of the car-ferry dock, and they just might be lucky enough to see a big car ferry unloading or loading railroad cars. This mating, as you might call it, of train and ship — *the* two means of transportation of the time — represented the epitome of progress.

Since the Door County Special had backed into Kewaunee, it was able to pull out of the station with the engine at the head of the train once more. The interlude of the brakeman's reign was past, and the back platform resumed its former function of catering to the few privileged to ride there.

There was a sort of let-down on the Door County Special after she left Kewaunee, for she steamed right on through Casco Junction and made only one more stop — at Luxembourg — on her way to Green Bay. After that, the trappings of baggage and coats and hats and magazines and everything else would be gathered in for the arrival at the Chicago and Northwestern Station. Cinders were dusted from children, and faces were washed, under protest. Generally, there was a hubbub of movement in the Door County Special.

The "Limited" arriving in Green Bay   ca 1913

Accessed by train, Green Bay always seemed much larger than the census said it was. Perhaps it was because the train crept very slowly through the industrial area, around many turns, and across a multitude of switches until, at last, the brakes gave their final squeal and the train came to rest at the station.

By the time all the passengers had disembarked on the Green Bay and Western side and moved across to the Chicago and Northwestern side of the platform, all the baggage had been removed and loaded onto four-wheeled carts, ready to be disgorged into the other train. The bags went into baggage cars if they were trunks, or into the hands of the porters in charge of the parlor cars, if they were handbags.

Then there was much waiting, much straining to see up the straight track toward Marinette until, finally, there it was. The Limited was in sight! It came hurtling up in a cloud of steam, a scream of brakes, and a shower of cinders. Such elegance! The parlor car seats were bigger and deeper and the windows wider. But, as one, the little boys and girls dove for the back platform with parents in hot pursuit. Some parents thought that one bath of cinders should be enough for one day, but some of the adults always stayed outside too — as many as there was room for.

It was past five now, and (electric) lights began to appear. The cluck of the rails became faster and more rhythmic, only to be broken at each crossing where there was a clanging bell to warn pedestrians, cars, and horse-drawn vehicles that the Chicago Northwestern Limited was passing through on its way to the big cities. The porter announced each station stop in a deep, resonant bass voice that gave wonderful emphasis to the names of the towns, like "Dee-Pee-ah," the town just south of Green Bay. But the only attraction capable of wooing the smaller people away from the back platform was the ultimate adventure in train travel — the dining car!

Dinner on the train was always an event. If you have never dined in the regal splendor of a dining car, particularly immediately after

Chambers Island and the Strawberry Islands   1928

two months in the woods of upper Door County; if you have never dined on the inimitable produce of Wisconsin — steak or chicken, ham or roast beef, big baked potato or potato salad, corn on the cob (especially corn on the cob!) — then you have missed something that will probably never come again. The diners of that era with all their epicurean delights have given way to fast-food service and the trays in airplanes.

Meanwhile, dusk was settling in on the sweeping fields ripe for harvest. One glorious evening scene after another swept past, punctuated by lights in farm houses replacing the light in the sky. The deep green of trees in their late summer finery turned black in the approaching night; great red barns rapidly became silhouettes; black and white cows stood munching serenely, content on their pastoral acres.

The resonant tones of "Dee-Pee-ah," the cluck of the rails, the clang of the crossing bells — they all marked the end of another summer, even the end of another time. The porter who called out the names of towns is gone, along with the Northwestern Limited, and the little girls and boys are old now, if they have not already gone to join the Limited and the porter.

And it is also true that the *Carolina*, Mike Anderson, the *Volunteer*, the Hillside Hotel, the old hooker *Lucille*, the fish house on the big dock, and the Door County Special are all gone too.

Yes, but those are my memories.

The peninsula is still there, the bays haven't changed, the sunsets are just as beautiful, and the storms are just as rousing. Some day the fish will be back in force, and belligerent small-mouth bass will lurk on the edge of the underwater ledge just waiting for a fight.

And one day you might reach the brink of that hill and see before you bays, bluffs, islands . . . to infinity. You might be seeing it for the first time. How wonderful that would be! You might drive north to

Dry bones of an ancient skiff 1978

Northport through Gills Rock and see Death's Door and be disappointed because the waves are not a mile high and tossing everything about. You could even cross the Door on the big, sturdy ferryboat and wonder why anyone was ever in awe of it.

You might even wonder if the Big Bluff really does look like God, and you could go and look at it, just to find out.

All the ingredients are there and probably always will be. It is the memories that have to be made.

Is thunder really spawned over Death's Door?

Indubitably!

INDEX